SEE

For Lisa-Marie and Mia. She will always
see and hear you. Love, T xx — TM

To my lovely sis, Anna, the beautiful lady I hear from
every day but don't get to see enough. — JR

IF I STOP A MOMENT, AND LOOK AROUND,

I CAN SEE SO MANY THINGS ...

CRAWLING SPOTS.

SQUIGGLY RAIN.

HEAVENLY HORSES.

A SLIPPERY FLICKER.

STORY LANDS.

FLYING
FEATHERS.

A **LONG-LOST** CHUM.

LACY
FLUTTERS.

GIFT-WRAPPED SURPRISE.

A HOME.

AND VERY, VERY BEST OF ALL, I CAN SEE ... THE ENDLESS STARS OF OUTER SPACE.

HUSHHHHHH . . .

AND VERY, VERY . . . BEST OF ALL, I CAN HEAR THE ENDLESS QUIET OF OUTER SPACE.

A SONG IN MY **HEART**.

TRA LA LAAA!

GIGGLE
GIGGLE
GIGGLE

HAPPINESS.

ZZZZZZZZZZB

BUZZING
BLOSSOMS.

A RUMBLING PURR.

PURR
PURR

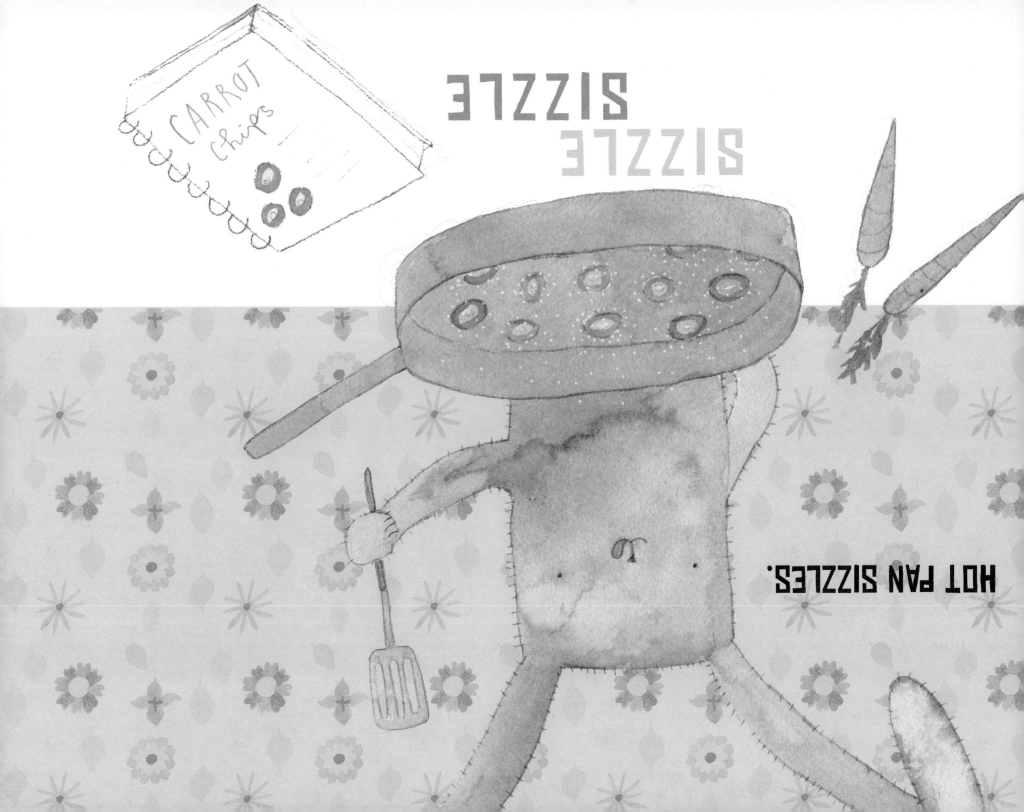

SIZZLE
SIZZLE

HOT PAN SIZZLES.

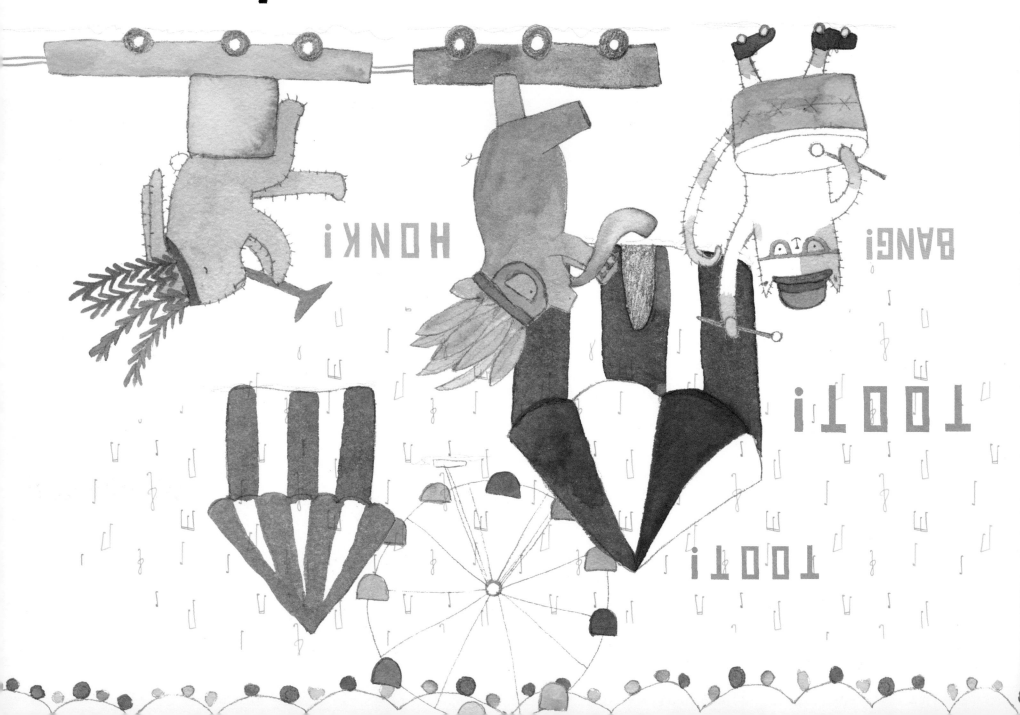

GLATTERING
BEADS.

GLATTER!
GLATTER!
GLATTER!
GLATTER!

SLIP!

THE TURN OF A PAGE.

POPPING SNACKS.

HAPPY HUMMING.

MMM HMM HMM HMM...

CHIRP!

TWEET!

TWEETS
IN A NEST.

IF I STOP A MOMENT, AND LISTEN HARD,

I CAN HEAR SO MANY THINGS ...

First published 2018

EK Books
an imprint of Exisle Publishing Pty Ltd
PO Box 864, Chatswood, NSW 2057, Australia
226 High Street, Dunedin, 9016, New Zealand
www.ekbooks.org

A CiP record for this book is available from the National Library of Australia.

ISBN 978-1-921966-67-5

Designed by Big Cat Design
Typeset in Chinese Rocks 27 on 35pt leading
Printed in China

This book uses paper sourced under ISO 14001 guidelines from well-managed forests and other controlled sources.

2 4 6 8 10 9 7 5 3 1

HEAR